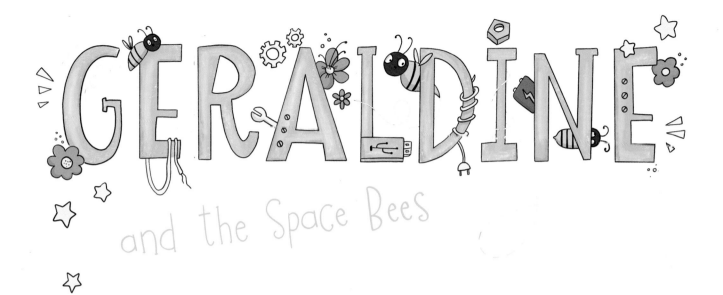

GERALDINE
and the Space Bees

Sol Regwan

Illustrated by Denise Muzzio

Schiffer **Kids**

4880 Lower Valley Road, Atglen, PA 19310

Geraldine was watering her mom's flowers, but something was definitely wrong.

"This is very strange! Where are the rest of the bees?"
she asked the two lonely bumblebees hovering above her head.

Usually there were swarms of bees. Geraldine had even worn her
makeshift beekeeper outfit—made
from Dad's old shirt and Mom's favorite lampshade.
What could be going on?

The next day at school, Mrs. Hedley had a special announcement, but Geraldine was barely listening. She was still thinking about the missing bees. Where were those pesky little insects? She would have to ask her mom after school.

Suddenly, she heard the words
"space museum" fly out of
Mrs. Hedley's mouth. Space museum?!
Now she was listening!

SPACE
MUSEUM

"That's right, Geraldine. I have planned a special field trip," repeated Mrs. Hedley. "We are going to the space museum."

Geraldine was excited. She stood up, threw her arms in the air, and shouted, "Yes, yes, yes!" Ever since she won the science contest with her spectacular telescopic eyeglasses, she had wanted to visit outer space—especially Mars.

The day of the field trip, Geraldine packed her
new 3-D camera into her backpack. She had made it herself
out of recycled plastic and old lenses.

She also packed her award-winning eyeglasses—just in case.

Everyone was fascinated as the tour guide, Mr. Carter, described what it is like to travel in outer space. "Floating in zero gravity feels amazing. One little push can send you gliding through the air," he explained to the group.

Then he led them through the exhibits. They saw an enormous rocket, two rocket boosters, a space shuttle engine, and a video of a rocket launch.

Geraldine was fascinated when Mr. Carter said
that scientists send plants and animals into space
to see how they adapt to space travel.

At the end of the tour, Mr. Carter announced that he had homework for the class. "Each of you will create a model of something you would like to send into outer space, and explain why."

"I would send an elephant," said Brayden, "to see if it would float."
"I would send a spider to see if it could spin a web," said Julianna.
"How about a cactus?" shouted Geraldine. "Would it grow
down instead of up?"

Mr. Carter told the class that he would come to their classroom in one week to see their projects.

That evening, Geraldine thought and thought. What would she most like to send into space? Then she remembered the bees. The bees!

Her mom had told her about the bee population
declining and that something called pesticides were to blame.
"That's it!" yelled Geraldine.

"I will build a device that will let bees travel into outer space." What if bees could survive in a spaceship without these chemicals?

Geraldine was now excited. If she couldn't go to Mars, maybe her bees could!

She hunted through her pile of gadgets. She would build a clean, pesticide-free feeding station for the bees that would help scientists learn why the bees were disappearing.

Rummaging through Dad's shed, Geraldine found an old wooden crate.
She filled it with dirt from her mom's pesticide-free garden and painted
the outside of the crate purple to attract the bees.

She carefully dug up some of Mom's flowers and replanted them
in the crate, then pressed several of Mom's teacups into the dirt;
they were just the right size for holding water. "Perfect!" she thought.
"The bees will have plenty of room to float around when
they become weightless."

Geraldine covered the crate with an old lace curtain and tied it with a pink ribbon. She set the box in her mother's garden, with the top slightly open so bees could find their way in.

The following week, as her classmates
displayed their projects, Geraldine was nervous.
She had only been able to capture two bees.

When it was Geraldine's turn to present, she took a deep breath and explained, "Bees are dying because of the pesticides used on flowers.

If bees can't pollinate the plants, our food supply will be affected. We have to do something! I would like to send bees into space so they can make more bees in a clean environment. We can raise a new generation of healthy bees and bring them back to Earth."

"What a clever invention,"
said Mr. Carter. "Can I use it as an
exhibit in the space museum?"
"Of course!" said Geraldine.

Mrs. Hedley was proud. So was Mr. Carter. Geraldine was very proud!

POLLINATION

Why are bees so important?

Pollen is a very fine powder that bees carry from one plant to another. This fertilizes the plants, helping them grow baby plants, called seedlings. Without pollination, we would not have as many flowers or foods available. That is why it is so important for scientists to find ways to save the bees.

Western honeybees are the most common of the 7-12 honeybee species worldwide. They are the most important pollinators globally and face threats and extinction that could be absolutely disastrous for our planet.

Look for the next book in the

series coming soon!

Cover design by Danielle D. Farmer
Type set in Hockey is Lif © Tom Murphy, courtesy of
Divide by Zero Fonts § www.fonts.tom7.com / Cover font
handdrawn by Denise Muzzio

ISBN: 978-0-7643-5994-1
Printed in China

Published by Schiffer Kids
An imprint of Schiffer Publishing, Ltd.
4880 Lower Valley Road
Atglen, PA 19310
Phone: (610) 593-1777; Fax: (610) 593-2002
E-mail: Info@schifferbooks.com
Web: www.schifferbooks.com

For our complete selection of fine books on this and related
subjects, please visit our website at www.schifferbooks.com.
You may also write for a free catalog.

Schiffer Publishing's titles are available at special discounts
for bulk purchases for sales promotions or premiums. Special
editions, including personalized covers, corporate imprints, and
excerpts, can be created in large quantities for special needs.
For more information, contact the publisher.

We are always looking for people to write books on new and
related subjects. If you have an idea for a book, please contact
us at proposals@schifferbooks.com.

Check out the first book in
the Gizmo Girl series:

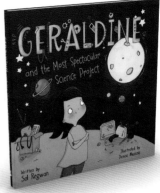

Geraldine is an energetic,
spirited second-grader with
dreams of becoming an
astronaut. She knows that
she's clever and inventive, but
can she create the winning
entry in her class science
contest? Armed with nothing
but her strong will and the
broken parts of her parents' old gadgets and gizmos,
she sets out to invent an amazing contraption. Will her
invention wow her classmates and transform her from
class troublemaker to creative scientist?

Geraldine and the
Most Spectacular Science Project
Sol Regwan,
Illustrated by Denise Muzzio
978-0-7643-5898-2

For my beautiful daughter, Olivia,
whose spunkiness and curiousity
inspires me every day.

—S. R.

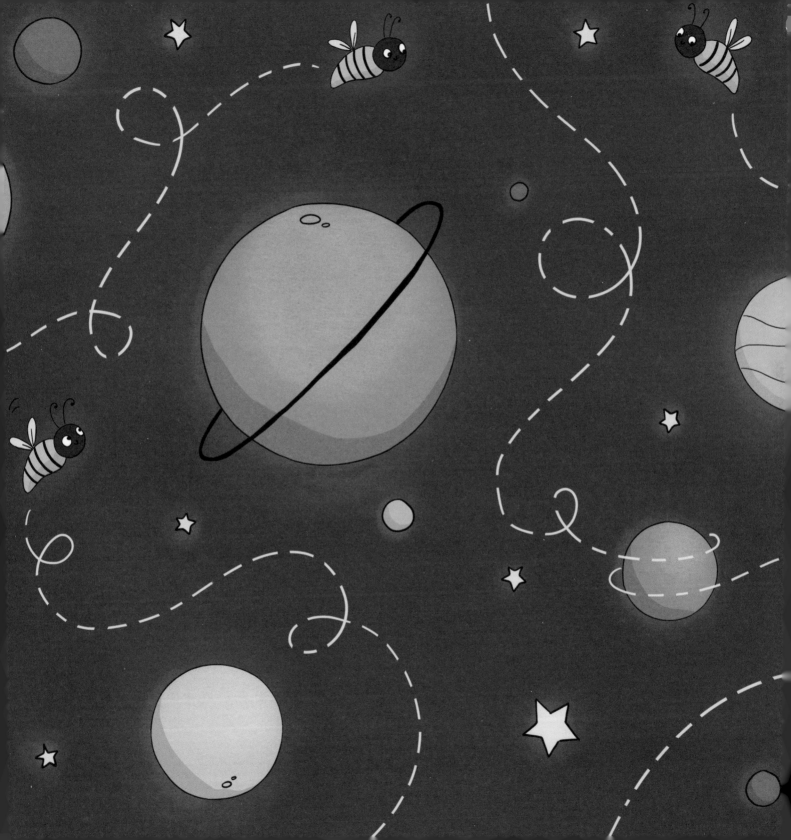